In Search of Lost Time
In the Shadow of Young Girls in Flower

Marcel Proust

In Search of Lost Time

In the Shadow of Young Girls in Flower

Adaptation and Drawings by
Stanislas Brézet and Stéphane Heuet

Translated by
Laura Marris

LIVERIGHT PUBLISHING CORPORATION
A Division of W. W. Norton & Company
Independent Publishers Since 1923

Copyright © 2000 by Guy Delcourt Productions
Copyright © 2002 by Éditions Delcourt
Translation copyright © 2020 by Laura Marris

Originally published in French as *À L'ombre des Jeunes Filles en Fleurs* parts 1 and 2 from
À la Recherche du Temps Perdu by Marcel Proust, adapted by Stanislas Brézet and Stéphane Heuet

For information about permission to reproduce selections from this book, write to
Permissions, Liveright Publishing Corporation, a division of W. W. Norton & Company, Inc.,
500 Fifth Avenue, New York, NY 10110

For information about special discounts for bulk purchases, please contact
W. W. Norton Special Sales at specialsales@wwnorton.com or 800-233-4830

Manufacturing by RR Donnelley, Shenzhen
Production manager: Anna Oler

Library of Congress Cataloging-in-Publication Data

Names: Brézet, Stanislas, adapter, illustrator. | Heuet, Stéphane, adapter, illustrator. |
Marris, Laura, 1987– translator. | Proust, Marcel, 1871–1922. A l'ombre des jeunes filles en fleurs.
Title: In the shadow of young girls in flower / Marcel Proust; adaptation and drawings
by Stanislas Brézet and Stéphane Heuet; translated by Laura Marris.
Other titles: A l'ombre des jeunes filles en fleurs. English Description: New York :
Liveright Publishing Corporation, a division of W. W. Norton & Company,
[2020] | Series: In search of lost time; [Volume 2] | "Originally published in French as
A l'ombre des jeunes filles en fleurs parts 1 and 2 from A la recherche du temps perdu
by Marcel Proust, adapted by Stanislas Brézet and Stéphane Heuet"
Identifiers: LCCN 2019022190 | ISBN 9781631493676 (pbk.)
Subjects: LCSH: Proust, Marcel, 1871–1922—Adaptations. | France—Social life and customs—
19th century—Comic books, strips, etc. | Graphic novels.
Classification: LCC PN6747.B75 A6613 2020 | DDC 741.5/944—dc23
LC record available at https://lccn.loc.gov/2019022190

Liveright Publishing Corporation, 500 Fifth Avenue, New York, N.Y. 10110
www.wwnorton.com

W. W. Norton & Company Ltd., 15 Carlisle Street, London W1D 3BS

1 2 3 4 5 6 7 8 9 0

TRANSLATOR'S INTRODUCTION

Around 1890, a young Marcel Proust filled out a questionnaire in a friend's "confession book," a popular type of album that was passed around social circles like a personality quiz. In response to the question "Where would you like to live?," Proust wrote, "A country where certain things I wish would come true as if by magic and where tenderness would always be returned."

Though he was not yet twenty, this answer offers a glimpse of the author's voice and the convex lens of yearning through which he examined the world. This questionnaire comes from a period of the author's life that runs parallel to the adolescent moment of *In the Shadow of Young Girls in Flower*, the second volume of Proust's masterwork, *In Search of Lost Time*. In this volume, the narrator gets over his first infatuation with Gilberte Swann and travels with his grandmother to the seaside town of Balbec, where he is both attracted to and intimidated by the group of young women he befriends. Chief among this girl-gang is Albertine, who will become the narrator's main love and torment in subsequent volumes, especially *The Prisoner* and *The Fugitive*. The poet Anne Carson condenses it well in *The Albertine Workout* when she writes, "The jealous lover cannot rest until he is able to touch all the points in space and time ever occupied by the beloved." Tenderness may be, in the Proustian

universe, the only antidote to possessiveness and jealousy.

At the moment of this volume, in the resort town of Balbec, the narrator and his friends are still insulated from the weight of adult passion. Balbec may not be the ideal country of Proust's questionnaire, but it is a tender space, full of delicately wrought images that the narrator will return to over and over, as the first sightings of Albertine and her friends come to symbolize the inexperience of these early encounters. As in many relationships, the earliest images of the beloved only snowball in their significance. In later volumes, the memory of young Albertine standing by the sea takes on another tenderness—that of pressing a bruise. Balbec, an intermediate place between childhood and adulthood, possesses a hyperreal quality that is only intensified by the graphic novel form of this excellent adaptation by Stanislas Brézet and Stéphane Heuet.

Balbec, which was modeled on the French town of Cabourg, unfolds vividly in the narrator's mind, saturating every aspect of his experience, almost as if he were dreaming it. Unlike the more speculative section "Place Names: The Name" that concludes *Swann's Way*, here the word is anchored to the world itself: "Place Names: The Place." In a process that is familiar to every traveler, the narrator confronts the differences between what he imagines Balbec to be and the place he ultimately discovers.

As always, Proust is tremendously sensitive to the shifting social and physical landscape. In her essay "The Weather in Proust," Eve Kosofsky Sedgwick calls both the narrator and his grandmother "human barometers" responding to the slightest change in pressure between interior life and exterior world. Their intergenerational communion is perhaps the most tenderly calibrated of all. When the narrator and his grandmother wake up in the morning, they communicate by knocking on the thin wall between their hotel rooms. Sedgwick calls this divider "as eloquent a membrane as if it demarcated the chambers of a single ear, or heart." This trip to Balbec is all the more poignant because it represents some of the last uninterrupted time the narrator and his grandmother will spend together before her death in volume 3. When the narrator next visits Balbec, he will be thinking through her loss, looking for a place where he can allow himself to be overwhelmed by his feelings of grief.

But in this volume, the narrator can focus on his experience of Balbec in all its initial freshness. In this time of relative innocence, he has no reason to fear his curiosity about the adult world and its enticements. Some readers may know this volume by its first English title, *Within A Budding Grove*, but that rendering leaves out the essential girls. The more literal version of the title, *In the Shadow of Young Girls in Flower*, captures the enveloping veil of the narrator's infatuation and his pleasure at being overshadowed and outmaneuvered by these girls as they play children's games on the bluff, familiar amusements whose gestures sud-denly take on new interest, offering a chance to flirt. These intoxicating afternoons are highly visual and tactile, especially in Heuet's excellent drawings. The cerebral narrator suddenly finds himself closely observing what interests his new friends, like the "vulgar" delights of the high season—dances at the casino, yachts, and horse races.

This shift in the narrator's perspective changed how I thought of the project as a whole. As Arthur Goldhammer aptly put it in the introduction to his translation of the first volume in this series, the graphic novel adaptation of *In Search of Lost Time* resembles "a piano reduction of an orchestral score." But, to me, Brézet and Heuet's version of *In the Shadow of Young Girls in Flower* evokes a more visual metaphor. If Proust's novel is a great tableau, this adaptation of the second volume is like a sketch that lays bare the gestures of the original masterpiece. This emphasis on sight is reflected by the opinions of Albertine, as she gradually becomes the animating force of the narrator's romantic obsession. He jokes about her terrible taste in music but notices that she speaks with authority about visual art.

Where volume 1 has the composer Vinteuil and the "little phrase" of his sonata, this volume has Elstir the painter and his drawings. On one of his walks with the narrator, Elstir compares his final painting, *Carquethuit Harbor*, to his sketch: "a little drawing where you can see the contours of the beach much more clearly." That sketch has something in common with this adaptation of Proust. Each sentence and speech bubble carries the weight of a contour, a defining mark that holds the experience together. Heuet's images create the flavor of Proust's descriptions in all their decadence, sustaining the force of the lines excerpted from the original.

As a translator, my primary challenge was to stay immersed in Proust's tone even in the shorter pieces of text. In these moments, there is little scaffolding for Proust's more baroque inclinations. The text of this adaptation has its own natural rhythm that builds as a reader's eye moves across the page. Brézet and Heuet have very gracefully intertwined Proust's sentences with the images, and I have done my best to keep the text in step with the drawings. This alignment meant that I could not rearrange the order of some phrases in a sentence, which I otherwise might have done, since I judged that these words were better served by their accompanying frames.

It bears noting some moments within these frames that may startle the contemporary reader—especially concerning the Baron de Charlus. Before the baron arrives in Balbec, Proust hears a terrible story about Charlus beating a prominent man almost to death because the man propositioned him. In fact, this story is likely an elaborate cover for Charlus' own queerness, which Proust depicts over the course of the volumes. Proust explained his characterization of Charlus in a letter to André Gide: "I tried to portray a homosexual infatuated with virility. . . . I don't in the least claim that he is the only type of homosexual. But he's an interesting type which, I believe, hasn't ever been described." As a teenager, Proust was open with his friends about his desire and affection for other boys, and from this early age, he defended gay and lesbian love as no less moral than love in straight relationships. The fact that the narrator's love interests have feminized male names (Gilbert, Albert) is a wink at this personal history. Albertine herself goes on to have affairs with women, which sparks the narrator's jealousy.

Another startling aspect of the story concerns the Jewish visitors to Balbec. One political undercurrent in this volume is the unfolding of the Dreyfus affair, which stemmed from the wrongful conviction of Alfred Dreyfus, a Jewish captain in the French army, who was condemned to prison and stripped of his rank in 1894 for supposedly selling military secrets to the Germans. Proust was an outspoken defender of Dreyfus, which set him against many members of French high society. In this volume, Proust frankly depicts the anti-Semitism of the haute-bourgeoisie and the aristocracy at the time, as well as the drama of social assimilation. Aimé, the manager of the hotel and a Romanian immigrant, tries to ingratiate himself with the narrator by saying that Dreyfus is "guilty a thousand times over," because he imagines that's what the narrator will want to hear. Proust's own relationship to Jewish culture is complex: though his mother was Jewish, he never formally practiced a religion—except, perhaps, the adoration of memory.

Yet it took Proust years to become the high priest of literary remembering. The prestigious publishing house Gallimard, on the advice of André Gide, initially rejected volume 1 of *In Search of Lost Time*, which Gide came to deeply regret. Proust sent the book to be published by Grasset at his own expense. *In the Shadow of Young Girls in Flower* was a breakthrough for Proust, since it was at last picked up by Gallimard and won the 1919 Prix Goncourt, France's most prestigious prize for a novel. And from there the world succumbed to the irresistible power of Proust's sense of observation, his portrait of a mind on the page. Even the questionnaire he innocently filled out in a friend's album has come to bear his name, lending this simple parlor game a prestige that has drawn celebrities from Lauren Bacall to Karl Ove Knåusgaard.

I'm grateful to the previous translators of Proust whose work I have consulted, and particularly to Arthur Goldhammer. This volume contains two flashbacks to volume I— Swann's comment about Balbec and the scene from the Verdurins' where M. Biche (aka Elstir) entertains the gathering in a way he regrets. I have reused snippets of Goldhammer's excellent translations of these moments to preserve the continuity between volumes of the graphic novel. I also want to thank Alice Kaplan for her sharp eye and her generous advice about the translation. Evelyne Bloch-Dano's *Une jeunesse de Marcel Proust* and Pauline Newman-Gordon's *Dictionnaire des idées dans l'oeuvre de Marcel Proust* were indispensable references. And thanks to Henry Sussman, whose brilliant, creative lectures were my first introduction to Proust.

Proust himself had a high regard for adolescence, especially its spontaneity. He wrote that it was a time when people can learn from observation, without the blinders of social norms. But Proust never lost this ability. Reynaldo Hahn, Proust's longtime lover, once described Proust stopping to examine a rosebush, entirely transfixed: "How many times I've observed Marcel in these mysterious moments in which he was communicating totally with nature, with art, with life, in these 'deep minutes' in which his entire being was concentrated." The mark of Proust's art was to stumble again and again on new visions of something familiar. I hope this rendering will be read in that spirit.

—Laura Marris

In Search of Lost Time

In the Shadow of Young Girls in Flower

Place Names: The Place

(Part One)

 had reached an almost complete indifference to Gilberte, when two years later, I left with my grand-mother for Balbec.

Hurry up! You're going to miss the 1:22 train!

For the first time, I felt it was possible that my mother could live without me, other than for me, could live another life.

Well, what would the church at Balbec say if she knew someone was planning to visit her with such a sorrowful air? What happened to Ruskin's delighted traveler?

Even from far away, I'll still be with you, my little man. You'll have a letter from your maman tomorrow.

My dear girl, you're like Madame de Sévigné, with a map before your eyes, following us at every moment.

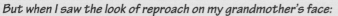

To avoid the suffocating fits traveling brought on, the doctor had advised me to drink a little too much beer or cognac just as we were leaving, so as to be in that state he called "euphoria," when the nervous system is temporarily less vulnerable.

But when I saw the look of reproach on my grandmother's face:

. . . you know what the doctor said— and this is the advice you give me!

Well in that case, be quick and get some beer or a brandy if it's supposed to do you good.

You'd better try to sleep for a bit.

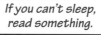

Marie de Rabutin-Chantal
MARQUISE
de
SÉVIGNÉ
Lettres

If you can't sleep, read something.

Contemplating the window shade seemed like an excellent thing . . .

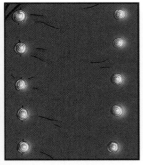

The pleasure I felt at studying the blue shade and feeling that my mouth was half-open began to dissipate. I became more mobile;

I began to stir a little and could choose to fix my attention on this or that page.

While I was reading I could feel my admiration grow for Mme de Sévigné . . .

. . . a great artist from the same family as Elstir, a painter I would meet in Balbec.

She presents things to us in the same way he does: in the order of our perceptions instead of first explaining them by their causes.

Since my grandmother could never bring herself to rush "willy-nilly" to Balbec, she would stop for the night at the home of one of her friends, but I left that same evening, so as not to trouble her,

CHUG A
CHUG A
CHUG A
CHUG A
CHUG

and so I could see the church at Balbec the following day.

Sunrises go hand in hand with long journeys by rail, as do hard-boiled eggs,
illustrated papers, games of cards, and rivers where barges strive but make no headway.

The train stopped at a little station. Nothing was visible against the backdrop of the gorge except a lone gamekeeper's cottage.

If a being could be a product of the soil, so that you tasted in that person all of its particular charms, then the tall girl who emerged from that cottage was just such a one.

In the valley, she must never see anyone except on these trains . . .

Faced with her, I felt a desire for life that is reborn in us each time we rediscover beauty and happiness.

Mademoiselle!

CHOOOO

SSHHHHHHHH

It was fully daylight now— the dawn was behind me.

ERTAIN names of towns, like Vézelay or Chartres, Bourges or Beauvais, serve to denote, by abbreviation, their principal church. Nevertheless, it was on a train station that I first read the almost Persian-style name of Balbec.

I do indeed know Balbec! The church in Balbec, which dates back to the twelfth and thirteenth centuries and is still half Romanesque, is perhaps the most curious specimen of Norman Gothic, and most unusual! You might mistake it for a work of Persian inspiration.

I asked the way to the shore, so I could see only the ocean and the church; people didn't seem to understand what I meant.

Of course, it was certainly in the sea where, according to the legend, the fishermen found the miraculous Christ, a discovery which was represented a few yards away in a stained-glass panel;

it was true that the nave and the towers were built from wave-battered stones. But this ocean, which I had imagined would exhaust itself at the foot of the glass, was more than five leagues away, at Balbec-Plage.

It's here—that's the Balbec church.

of these Apostles, that famous Virgin in the entranceway,

I thought to myself: "All I have seen, until now, are photographs of this church, and

only plaster casts.

Now that this is the real church, the real statue, it's much more."

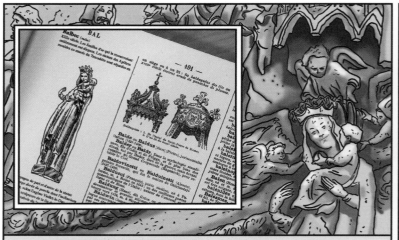

And perhaps also less. My imagination was astonished to see this statue it had sculpted a thousand times reduced to its original appearance in stone,

. . . subjected to the tyranny of the Particular.

The hour was slipping away—I had to return to the station, to wait for my grandmother.

It's delicious, as beautiful as Sienna.

Well, how was Balbec?

I didn't dare divulge my disappointment.

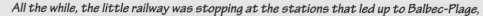

All the while, the little railway was stopping at the stations that led up to Balbec-Plage,

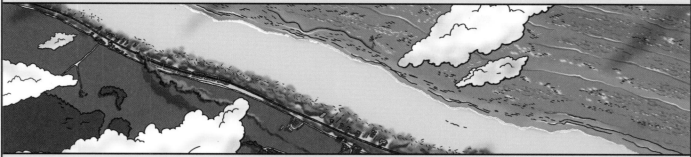

little stations that for the first time revealed their usual hosts to me,
but revealed them by their exteriors . . . which cruelly hurt, with their images both strangely ordinary
and disdainfully familiar, my unknown looks and my homesick heart.

INCARVILLE

MARCOUVILLE

DOVILLE

PONT-À-COULEUVRE

ARAMBOUVILLE

SAINT-MARS-LE-VIEUX

HERMONVILLE

MAINEVIL[LE]

BALBEC

But how my suffering grew when we reached the lobby of the Grand Hotel de Balbec!

GRAND HÔTEL

And what are . . . your rates?

Even in this palace, there were people who,
being esteemed by the proprietor, didn't pay very much,
on the condition that he could be certain . . .

. . . they refrained from spending not out of poverty, but out of stinginess. That characteristic could do nothing to tarnish prestige, since it is a vice and could appear in any social class.

Um . . . I don't feel well. I think we may have to go back to Paris.

I'm going out to do some errands.

Any letters for me?

If Monsieur would like to follow me . . .

Social class was the only thing the manager paid attention to, social class,
or rather, signs that seemed to indicate its loftiness.

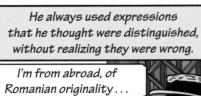

He always used expressions that he thought were distinguished, without realizing they were wrong.

I'm from abroad, of Romanian originality . . .

All good? Settling in?

And don't hesitate to knock on the wall if you need anything tonight. My bed is just across the wall from yours, the partition is very thin.

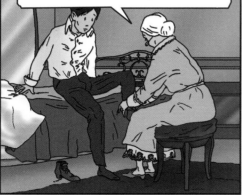

That first night of arrival, when my grandmother left me, I began to suffer, as I had already suffered in Paris upon leaving the house.

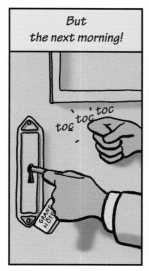

But the next morning!

toc toc toc

Good morning, monsieur.

What joy, to already think of a pleasing lunch, and of the promenade, of seeing, in the window and in all the glass panels of the cabinets, like in the portholes of a ship's cabin,

the naked sea . . .

I would stand in front of this window every morning, peering as if from the pane of a coach I had slept in, to see if during the night, a desired chain of hills has come closer or stretched further away—here, these hills of the sea . . .

VLAM

Since we were newcomers, the proprietor led us, under his protection, to our table at lunchtime, like an officer leading two recruits to the quartermaster to get them in uniform.

Aimé, this little fish you have here seems quite commendable: we'll have that, and a generous portion.

I see you're well taken care of.

In Combray, since everyone knew us, I did not bother with anyone.
In the life of seaside resorts, people do not know their neighbors.

I have it on good authority that this modern young man is mortifying his parents.

Apparently he gambles enormous sums at Baccarat, sums he can't afford to lose.

I was not yet old enough, and I still remained too sensitive to give up the desire to please others and to possess them. I did not have the noble indifference a man of society would have felt toward the people lunching in the dining room, or the boys and young girls passing by on the promenade.

I mistakenly gave you the table reserved for Monsieur Stermaria and his daughter.

Make sure it doesn't happen again . . .

Set table 7!

A little air will do you good.

clic

Sustained by the celestial breeze, my grandmother was as calm and cheerful as Saint Blandine in the middle of the insults that rallied against us, heightening my sense of melancholy and isolation . . .

... from the contemptuous tourists, mussed and furious. A group of them was made up of eminent persons from the major departments of that part of France.

The presiding judge from Caen...

The president of the Cherbourg bar...

An important notary from Mans...

They affected an attitude of scornful irony towards a Frenchman everyone called "Majesty," and who was, in truth, the self-proclaimed king of a little rock in Oceania, inhabited by a few savages.

He lived in the hotel, with his pretty mistress.

Long live the queen!

What a zoo!

It's truly a scourge, it makes you want to leave France!

Make no mistake: she's a working girl...

But someone swore to me that they used the royal cabin at Ostende!

Of course! You can rent it for twenty francs!

On the other hand, the president of the bar and his friends never ran out of sarcastic remarks about a rich, titled old woman who never went anywhere without her entire household staff.

Madame la Marquise, we have reserved our best room, which is unworthy of you...

Of course, the microcosm surrounding the old woman was not poisoned by virulent bitterness like this circle where the wives of the notary and the judge grimaced with rage.

13

I would have liked to be noticed by a man with a sloping forehead, his eyes shifting between his prejudices and his breeding, a great lord of the country, who was none other than Legrandin's brother-in-law. He sometimes came to visit Balbec, and on Sundays, the weekly garden party he and his wife hosted caused the hotel to empty of some of its inhabitants, because one or two among them would be invited to these parties, and because the rest, not wanting to seem like they had been left out, would choose that day for a far-flung excursion.

Look at that man over there, he's taking off his hat!

Yes ... surely a man out of the ordinary!

Monsieur le Marquis, we are so honored that you have accepted our hospitality.

Alas, among all these people, no one's scorn was as painful to me as M. de Stermaria's. For I had noticed his daughter as soon as she walked in.

The laws of heredity had given that complexion of choice juices the flavor of an exotic fruit or a famous vintage.

Yet all of a sudden a stroke of luck offered my grandmother and me the chance to gain immediate prestige in the eyes of all the hotel patrons.

I could tell the marquise was a prestigious person in the hotel, and her friendship could raise our standing in the eyes of M. de Stermaria.

The Marquise de Villeparisis.

In a few moments, I would cross these infinite social distances, which, at least at Balbec, separated me from Mademoiselle de Stermaria.

Not that my grandmother's friend seemed the least bit aristocratic to me—I had grown too accustomed to her name.

Unfortunately, my grandmother had a rule against socializing during travel; she thought one did not go to the seaside to visit with people,

... that it made you lose precious time better spent in the open air, by the waves, and finding it convenient to assume that this opinion was shared by everyone, and that it permitted, between two old friends, the fiction of a reciprocal anonymity, she merely turned her eyes away and seemed not to see Mme de Villeparisis, who, understanding that my grandmother did not want to recognize her, also looked away, into the air.

That evening . . .

They are the de Cambremers, aren't they? She's a marquise. And genuine. Not by marriage.

Oh! She's a very unassuming woman, she's charming, never puts on airs.

Aimé, you can tell M. de Stermaria that he's not the only noble to have graced your dining room.

The next day . . .

Our mutual friends, the de Cambremers rightly want to introduce us . . .

As always, but more easily while her father stepped away to chat with the president of the bar, I gazed at Mlle de Stermaria.

At certain looks that welled for a brief instant in the depths of her pupils, in which you could feel the almost humble softness a prevailing taste for sensual pleasures lends to the proudest women, looks that would soon respond only to a certain cachet, the one she saw in each being who could make her experience those pleasures, be it an actor or a circus performer, for whom she might someday leave her husband—at a certain vivid and sensual shade of pink that spread across her pale cheeks, like the shade that lends its crimson to the heart of the white water lilies of Vivonne, I believed she might have readily allowed me to seek out a taste of the very poetic life she was leading in Brittany.

But soon I had to turn my eyes away from Mlle de Stermaria, since her father had taken his leave of the president of the bar and returned to sit across from her, rubbing his hands like a man who has just acquired something precious.

As intimidating as these meals always were, they became even more so with the arrival, for several days, of the owner (or the general manager, I don't know which) of not only this palace, but also seven or eight others situated in every corner of France.

Once, when I stepped out at the beginning of dinner, I passed him as I returned, and he greeted me,

but with coldness, whose cause could have been either his reserve or his scorn for an unimportant patron.

Before those who had great standing . . .

He obviously saw himself as more than a director: an orchestra conductor, or a true generalissimo.

I could tell that even the movements of my spoon had not escaped him, and if he vanished after the soup course, his passing review made me lose my appetite for the rest of dinner. His own taste was quite hearty,

. . . as we saw him at lunch, which he took like an ordinary individual.

The other manager, the usual one, was constantly on his feet.

He tried to flatter him, and was terrified of his presence.

You deserve the ribbing of the commander of the Légion of Honor!

When the concierge, surrounded by his bellhops, told me:

He leaves for Dinard tomorrow morning. From there he'll go to Biarritz, and then to Cannes.

. . . I could breathe more easily.

In the end, we did socialize, thanks to my grandmother in spite of herself, when one morning she and Mme de Villeparisis bumped into each other in a doorway and were forced to greet each other.

And the marquise became accustomed to sitting with us for a moment every day while she was waiting to be served in the dining room.

Mme de Villeparisis has brought us some magnificent fruit.

I'm like you, I'm wild for fruit more than any other dessert.

I can't say, like Mme de Sévigné, that if on some whim we wanted bad fruit, we would be obliged to order it from Paris.

She appreciated it even more because the fruit they served at the hotel was generally detestable.

Ah, yes, you're reading Mme de Sévigné. From the first day, I saw you with her *Letters*. Don't you find it a bit exaggerated, this constant worry about her daughter? She talks about it too much to be sincere. She's not natural.

My grandmother found this line of discussion unhelpful.

17

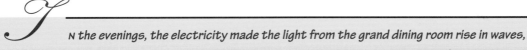

N the evenings, the electricity made the light from the grand dining room rise in waves,

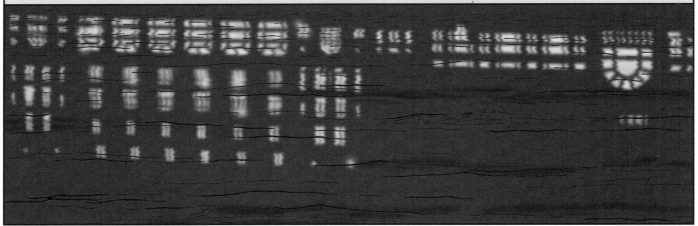

. . . the hall becoming an immense aquarium, where, in front of the glass partition, the working-class population of Balbec, the fishermen and the families of shopkeepers, invisible in the shadows, pressed themselves against the glass . . .

. . . to glimpse, slowly swaying in eddies of gold, the luxurious life of these people, as extraordinary to the poor as the lives of strange mollusks or fish.

It was a large social question—knowing whether the glass partition
would always protect these feasting, marvelous creatures, or if the shadowy figures
watching avidly in the night would not be tempted to harvest them from their aquarium and eat them.

Waiting there among the crowd, sequestered and entangled with the night,
there might have been some writer, some amateur of human ichthyology, who, watching the jaws
of these old feminine monsters gobbling a morsel of cuisine, would indulge himself in classifying
this one by race, by innate characteristics, and by acquired ones that made an old Serbian woman's
buccal appendage like that of a large ocean fish, because since her infancy she'd lived
in the fresh waters of the Faubourg Saint-Germain, eating salad like a La Rochefoucauld.

On several days, we saw the Princess of Luxembourg—pompously attended, tall, rosy, beautiful, with a bit of a strong nose—who was vacationing in the area for a few weeks.

Oh! Pish-posh. Would you look at that?

She would go out every morning to stroll on the beach at about the time everyone was returning for lunch after a dip. Even in her efforts to avoid putting on airs which might elevate her above us, she had poorly calculated the distance, since . . .

. . . I could feel the moment approaching when she would pat us as if we were two gentle beasts . . .

. . . who had slipped our heads toward her through the bars of a menagerie.

This is for your grandmother.

You'll eat some and give some to your grandmother to eat as well.

That was my first Highness.

When, due to a bout of fever, the Balbec doctor was called and recommended that I should not spend all day by the sea,

. . . my grandmother took his orders with an obvious respect, in which I perceived her firm decision not to follow a single one, but she did heed some matters of hygiene, and accepted Mme de Villeparisis' offer to take us on a few excursions in her carriage.

Mme de Villeparisis harnessed up at an early hour, so that we could have time to go as far as St-Mars-le-Vêtu, or all the way to the rocks of Quetteholme, or to some other excursion destination which, for a rather slow carriage, was quite a far distance, and required the whole day.

If it was Sunday, her carriage wasn't the only one in front of the hotel;

. . . several rented cabs awaited not only the guests invited to the chateau de Féterne by Mme de Cambremer, but also those who, not wanting to stay home like punished children, declared that Sunday was a tedious day in Balbec and left right after breakfast to hide at a nearby beach or to visit some interesting site.

Giddyup!

. . . It's like Stendhal's novels, which you seem to admire . . .

. . . my father, who saw him at the home of M. Mérimée—that man had talent, at least—

and, as M. Sainte-Beuve said, and mind you, he was very intelligent, you must believe those who have seen them up close . . .

The day Mme de Villeparisis took us to Carqueville . . .

You can find us at the baker's.

As I was leaving the church . . .

Might you be willing to run a little errand for me? I have to go find a bakery, but I don't know where it is. A carriage is waiting for me.

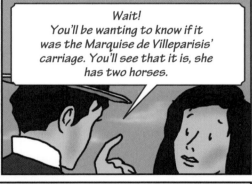
Wait! You'll be wanting to know if it was the Marquise de Villeparisis' carriage. You'll see that it is, she has two horses.

But when I pronounced the words "marquise" and "two horses," suddenly I sensed a great relief. It seemed like I had touched her body with invisible lips, and that I had pleased her. And this powerful grip on her spirit, that immaterial possession, had removed her mystery as much as if the possession had been physical.

We continued on toward Hudmesnil . . .

All of a sudden I was filled with that deep joy
which I had not often felt since leaving Combray, a joy like the one
that the steeples of Martinville, among others, had given me.

But
this time,
it remained incomplete.

I had just glimpsed three trees
which marked the entrance to a covered walkway

and formed a design
I had seen somewhere before.

I could not recognize the place they had detached themselves from,
but I could feel that it had once been familiar.

Where had I seen them before?
There were no walkways near Combray
that opened like this.

Soon, at a crossroads, the carriage left them behind. It led me far from the only thing I believed to be true,
what had truly made me happy; the carriage resembled my life.

We'll ask the coachman
to take the old road to Balbec—
it's so lovely!

What a dreamer you are . . .

As the trees became smaller, waving their desperate branches,
they seemed to say: "What you do not learn from us today, you will never know.
If you let us drop by the wayside of this road where we have tried to hoist ourselves to you,
a whole part of yourself, what we bring you, will fall forever into the void."

Did you go to the de Cambremers'?

No, we were at the Bec waterfalls.

I'm jealous, I would have liked to switch with you, it would have been an interesting alternative.

I was ravenous. And sometimes, to avoid delaying our meal,
I did not go upstairs to my room, and we waited all together in the hall
for the hotel proprietor to come tell us that dinner was served.

We're taking advantage of you.

How do you mean! I'm delighted, this is wonderful.

Each night, I would bring her the sketches I had made during the day of all those nonexistent beings who were not her.

One time...

I couldn't live without you.

But don't say such things!

clac

Our hearts must be harder than that. Otherwise, what would become of you if I went on a trip? I hope that on the contrary, you'd be very sensible and very happy.

I would be sensible if you left for a few days, but I would count the hours.

But if I left for months ... for years ... for ...

Her suffering caused me more pain than my own.

You know what a creature of habit I am. The first days I'm separated from the people I love most, I'm unhappy. But without loving them any less, I become accustomed, my life becomes calm, sweet; I can bear to be apart from them for months, years...

But the next day...

It's curious, after the latest scientific discoveries, materialism seems ruined. The most likely answer is once again the eternity of souls and their future reunion.

Ah, dear friends...

27

My nephew, in preparation for Saumur, is garrisoned nearby at Doncières. He's coming to spend his few weeks of break with me. I won't be able to see you as often.

During our excursions, she had praised his great intelligence, and especially his good heart; already I imagined that he would take a liking to me, that I would be his favorite companion. Before he arrived, his aunt let it be known that, unfortunately, he had fallen into the clutches of a depraved woman he was wild about, who wouldn't let him go. I was convinced that this kind of love would end fatally with mental alienation, crime, and suicide.

One very hot afternoon . . .

It's the young Marquis de Saint-Loup-en-Bray! What elegance!

Did you read in the paper? The description of his suit at the duel with the young Duke of Uzès!

It was that nephew of Mme de Villeparisis, the one she'd spoken to us about.

A letter for Monsieur Marquis!

Let's go!

What disappointment I felt in the following days when I realized that he didn't make an effort to come near us or even greet us in passing.

These icy manners were a far cry from the charming letters that just a few days earlier, I was imagining he would write to express his kindness toward me.

One day when I ran into them both, she was forced to introduce me to him.

When he slipped me his card the next day, I thought that he must, at the very least, be writing to propose a duel.

But he spoke to me about nothing but literature, and declared, after a long chat, that he very much desired to spend several hours each day with me.

I watched this disdainful person become the most amiable, the most considerate young man I had ever met.

He passed whole hours studying Nietzsche and Proudhon.

I hope my nephew isn't boring your grandson to death with his socialist speeches!

He was one of those "intellectuals," quick to admire, who shut themselves up in a book, caring only for elevated thoughts.

All the same, The Charterhouse is something major! . . .

It was decided very quickly between us that we had become great friends for life.

Our friendship is the greatest joy in my life, apart from my love for Rachel, of course.

These words provoked a sort of sadness, and I was embarrassed to respond, because I could not manage to find, in chatting with him (and it would have been the same with any other), the least bit of that happiness which it was possible for me to feel in solitude. When I had spent several hours talking with Robert de Saint-Loup, I felt a kind of remorse, regret, fatigue of not having been alone and ready, finally, to work.

When I discovered lingering in him that earlier, age-old being, that aristocrat Robert rightly aspired not to be, I felt a vivid happiness, but from intelligence, not friendship.

It was because he was a gentleman that his mental pursuits, his socialist

aspirations, which made him seek out pretentious, uncouth young students, had, for him, something pure and disinterested which they lacked among their own.

Believing himself descended from an ignorant and egotistical class,

he sincerely asked them to pardon his aristocratic origins, which, on the contrary, made them feel a kind of seduction. In this way, he started to make connections with people

which my parents, faithful to the sociology of Combray, would have been shocked to see him cultivate.

One day . . .

You can't even take two steps without running into one . . .

. . . I am not hostile, in principle, to the Jewish community, but here there are so many . . .

. . . you hear nothing but: "Say, Afraham, eye zaw Jakop . . ."

We looked up at this anti-Semite.

You'd think you were on the rue Aboukir.

But that's Bloch!

Bloch? I wonder if he'll remember me from exam day and the Université Populaire.

It was most amusing to rediscover the lessons of the Jesuits in the discomfort Robert felt whenever he feared he'd given offense.

Bloch wasn't alone at Balbec, unfortunately,
but with his sisters who had many friends and family.

Albert!

Albert!

In Balbec, as in certain countries
like Russia or Romania, geography courses

teach us that the Hebrew population
does not enjoy nearly the same favor
and has not arrived at the same degree
of assimilation, as it has in Paris, for example.

Of course, it's likely that this group, like all others, and perhaps even more than any other, must include many considerations, qualities, and virtues. But to understand them, one would have to be allowed in. But this group was not popular, and could feel it, and saw in this the proof of an anti-Semitism which it steeled itself against like a close, compact phalanx where no one from the outside could hope to penetrate.

Bloch introduced me to his sisters.

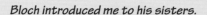

Come, close up these fair-clasped tunics of yours,
what's all this fuss about?

I'll bet you're at Balbec
to make some grand
acquaintances.

I had told him
that this trip
corresponded
with one of
my deepest
desires, though
less profound
than that
of going to
Venice . . .

Yes, of course, to sip sorbets with the lovely
madames, all the while pretending to read the *Stones
of Venayce* by Lord John Ruskin, musty bore and one
of the most plodding old fellows who ever lived.

Bloch apparently believed that not only
were all the male individuals in England lords,
but also that the letter "i" was always pronounced "ay."

Have you developed a taste for social climbing? Is that makes you spend time with Saint-Loup-en-Bray?

You must be suffering from a fine attack of snobbishness.

Tell me, are you a snob? You are, aren't you?

If I was a snob, I wouldn't spend time with you . . .

You're not very nice.

Pardon me, I've embarrassed you, tortured you, I've been wicked in my delight. And you can't imagine, that I, who've teased you so cruelly, hold such tenderness for you. Often, when I think of you, it brings me nearly to tears.

Believe me, and may the dark Fury seize me this instant and make me enter the gates of Hades, horrible to man, if yesterday, in thinking of you, I did not sob away half the night.

Albert, it's your turn!

These words, which I felt were made up in an instant, were not given much weight by his sermon "may the dark Fury." For Bloch, the Hellenic creed was strictly literary.

All these diatribes ended with an invitation to dinner.

My dear master Albert, and you, beloved cavalier of Arès, de Saint-Loup-en-Bray, breaker of horses, since I met you on the banks of the nymph Amphitrite, echoing with sea-foam, would you both like to come to dinner, one weeknight, at the home of my illustrious father with an impeccable heart?

He offered us this invitation because he wanted to tie himself more tightly to Saint-Loup, so that he would help him, he hoped, make his way in aristocratic circles.

But we had to put off the dinner because Saint-Loup couldn't leave—
he was waiting for an uncle who was coming to spend forty-eight hours with Mme de Villeparisis.

Saint-Loup spoke to me about his uncle's youth, now long past. Every day, he would bring women to a bachelor's apartment he kept with two of his friends who were as handsome as he was,

so that everyone called them "the three graces."

One day, one of the most prominent men in the Faubourg Saint-Germain asked my uncle to meet him at this bachelor apartment.

But as soon as he arrived, it wasn't to a woman, but to my uncle Palamède that he addressed his declaration.

My uncle pretended not to understand, and brought his two friends in under a pretext. They returned, grabbed the guilty man, undressed him, beat him bloody,

. . . and in ten-degrees-below-freezing weather, kicked him out the door . . .

. . . where he was found, close to death, so much so that the police made an investigation, and the poor man had all the trouble in the world convincing them to call it off.

It seemed hard to imagine how he set the tone, how he made the laws of society in his youth.

As handsome as he was, he must have had many women!

The next morning . . .

Tchac
Tchac
Tchac

pom ♩♪ . . . popom ♪♩ . . . pom

Pffffff . . . .

I had the impression of seeing a hotel crook.

His unusual expression made me take him for a thief if not a lunatic.

34

An hour later . . .

. . . I saw Mme de Villeparisis going out with Robert de Saint-Loup and the newcomer.

Quick as a flash, his look passed over me and away, as if he'd never seen me, focusing just in front of him, a bit downward, dulled . . .

I noticed he had changed his suit.

It seemed that if color was absent from his clothing, he had not banished it out of indifference, but rather because, for some unknown reason, he would not allow himself to wear it.

May I present my nephew, the Baron de Guermantes.

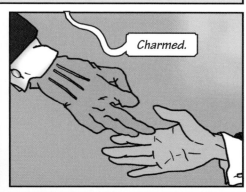

Charmed.

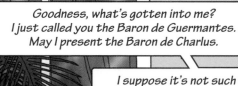

Goodness, what's gotten into me? I just called you the Baron de Guermantes. May I present the Baron de Charlus.

I suppose it's not such a big mistake— you are a Guermantes after all.

Saint-Loup's uncle didn't bother to say a word to me, or even glance my way.

Tell me, did I hear her right? Did Madame de Villeparisis say that your uncle is a Guermantes?

But of course, he is Palamède de Guermantes.

Those same Guermantes who have a chateau near Combray, who claim to be descended from Geneviève de Brabant?

Why, of course. The owner of the chateau is his brother.

His title is the Baron de Charlus.

I could now recognize, in the hard look he gave me when I saw him just outside the casino, the one I had seen him fix on me at Tansonville, at the moment when Mme Swann had called to Gilberte.

But isn't it true that he counts Mme Swann among his numerous mistresses?

Oh! Certainly not! He's a great friend of Swann and has always been very solicitous toward him. But it's never been said that he was his wife's lover.

In front of the Grand Hotel, the three Guermantes took their leave of us.

After dinner, I'm taking tea in my aunt Villeparisis' room. I hope you will give us the pleasure of your company, and your grandmother's.

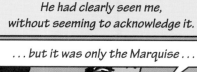
The nearness of the woman was enough . . .

. . . all of a sudden I thought: Oh! Good god! They've emptied the latrine . . .

He had clearly seen me, without seeming to acknowledge it.

. . . but it was only the Marquise . . .

I was quite astonished to see that Mme de Villeparisis, while happy to see us, did not seem to be expecting our arrival.

. . . who had just opened her mouth.

Ah! It was such a good idea for you to come by—it's charming, isn't it, Aunt?

But Monsieur! Don't you remember? It was you who asked us to come by this evening.

It was you, don't you remember?

If not for those eyes,
M. de Charlus' face would probably have resembled the faces of many handsome men.

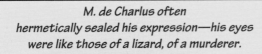

M. de Charlus often hermetically sealed his expression—his eyes were like those of a lizard, of a murderer.

On the whole, Mme de Sévigné has less to complain of than others. She spent a large part of her life near to what she loved.

I would have liked to guess what secret he carried that other men lacked, what had given M. de Charlus such a mysterious look when I had seen him that morning by the casino.

You're forgetting that it's not about love, but about her daughter.

His voice lingered on elevated notes,

The important thing in life is not what you love—it's the act of loving.

. . . taking on an unexpected softness, and seeming to contain a choir of fian-cées, of sisters, which overflowed with their tenderness.

What Mme de Sévigné feels for her daughter can much more justly claim to resemble the passion Racine depicts in *Andromache* or even *Phèdre* than the banal relationships the young Sévigné has with his mistresses.

Do you like *Andromache* and *Phèdre* very much?

There is more truth in one of Racine's tragedies than there is in all the dramas of Victor Hugo!

To prefer Racine over Victor, that alone is something major!

He told us that a home which had belonged to his family, where Marie-Antoinette had once slept, whose gardens were done by Le Nôtre, now belonged to rich, Jewish financiers, who had bought it.

For the home of the Guermantes to belong to Israel!

Israel, at least that's what these people call themselves, which seems to me to be more of a generic, ethnic term than a proper name.

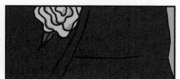

Can you imagine that the first thing they did was destroy the gardens by Le Nôtre, which is tantamount to slashing one of Poussin's canvasses. For that alone, these Israels should be in prison.

And of course there are probably many other reasons why they should be in there!

A bit later . . .

Toc
Toc

It's Charlus, may I come in Monsieur?

Monsieur, my nephew told me a moment ago that you are a bit troubled before bed, and what's more, you admire Bergotte's books. Since I had a book of his in my trunk that you probably have not read, I've brought it to help you pass these unhappy moments.

My discomfort as night approaches must seem stupid to you.

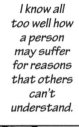

Not at all. You may not be exceptional—so few people are! But for a time at least, you have your youth, and that is always attractive.

I know all too well how a person may suffer for reasons that others can't understand.

. . .

I have another volume of Bergotte here.

I'll have it brought to you.

Go bring me your manager. He's the only one here who can run an errand properly.

Monsieur Aimé, Monsieur?

I don't know his name, but yes, I recall overhearing him called Aimé. Go quickly, I'm in a hurry!

He'll be here straightaway, Monsieur. I just saw him downstairs.

A certain time passed. The bellhop came back.

Monsieur, M. Aimé has gone to bed. But I can run your errand.

No, you just need to wake him up.

But I can't Monsieur, he doesn't sleep here.

In that case, leave us be.

But, Monsieur, you are too kind— one volume of Bergotte will be plenty.

That seems right, after all.

Good night, Monsieur.

Bang!

The next day, which was the day of his departure . . .

Your grandmother is waiting for you as soon as you're out of the water.

But you don't give a damn about your old grandmother do you, you little rascal!

?!

How can you say that, Monsieur? I adore her!

Monsieur, you are still young, and it would behoove you to learn two things: the first is to abstain from expressing feelings that are too obvious, lest they acquire unwelcome implications; the second is to avoid going to battle over the things people say to you without first understanding their meaning. If you had taken that precaution a moment ago, you would have avoided speaking drivel like an idiot while committing the additional absurdity of having anchors embroidered on your bathing costume.

I lent you a book by Bergotte which I need. Have it brought to me in an hour by that manager with the ridiculous and undeserved name, who, I imagine, is not asleep at this hour.

You've made me realize that, last night, I spoke too soon about the attractions of youth—I would have done better by you to warn of its indolence, its inconsequence, and its confusions.

I hope, Monsieur, that this little shower will be as beneficial as your dip.

But don't stand so still, you'll catch a cold. Good evening, Monsieur.

He must have regretted his words, since a little while later I received—in a Moroccan leather binding, whose front had been embossed with a branch of forget-me-not—the book he had lent me and which I had returned to him, not by Aimé, who was "out" but by the elevator boy.

By the way, who was that excellent apparition in the black getup I saw you walking with on the beach the day before yesterday?

That's my uncle.

My compliments, I should have guessed. He's extremely chic and has the priceless stance of an old bat of the finest breeding!

43

*T*HAT day, and the days before, Saint-Loup had to go to Doncières.

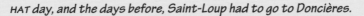
I was standing by myself in front of the Grand Hotel when I saw five or six young girls approaching whose manners and fashions set them apart from everyone I was accustomed to seeing in Balbec.

Were these anything but noble and serene models of human beauty, standing before the ocean, like sun-drenched statues on some shore of ancient Greece?

I'll go get you a newspaper.

That poor old man, he makes me sad, he seems just about done in.

From this vantage, their charming features
were no longer melded and confused.

I did not suppose
they could possibly be virtuous.

Never among actresses, or country girls, or young ladies in religious pensions had I ever seen anything
so beautiful, so full of the unknown, so completely precious, so truly inaccessible.

It was impossible to find a collection of rarer
specimens than these young flowers who,
in an instant, formed a delicate hedge
between my eyes and the horizon of waves.

I wondered if these young women
lived in Balbec, and who they might be . . .

To be
continued . . .

Place Names:
The Place

(Part Two)

She's a friend of young Simonet's.

I went in because I was planning to dine with Robert at Rivebelle that night, and on those evenings my grandmother required me to lie down for an hour before I left.

Without the shyness or melancholy of my first evening there . . .

I rang for the lift boy, who was no longer silent while I rose next to him in the elevator, like a mobile rib cage traversing the spinal column.

And on each floor a golden glow reflected on the carpet, announcing the sinking sun and the window of the restrooms.

Do you know of a Simonet family, here in Balbec?

I do seem to have heard talk of that name.

Have someone bring me the arrivals list.

Ever since, I have often tried to remember how the name Simonet had stood out to me on the beach. I do not know why, from the very first day, I guessed Simonet must be the name of one of those girls.

I entered my room.

As the season progressed, it changed the tableau I found in my window.

I was surrounded by images of the sea on all sides, as if I were stretched out on a bunk in one of the boats I could see passing quite close by.

Without saddening, without regretting it,
I let my usual dinner hour die away at the top of the curtains,
for I knew that this day was different from the others.

I knew the chrysalis of this dusk was preparing
to reveal, through a radiant metamorphosis,
the sparkling lights of the Rivebelle restaurant.

Time to go.

It's Aimé, Monsieur.

I have the arrivals list.

Before he left, Aimé insisted on telling me that
Dreyfus was guilty a thousand times over.

We'll know the whole story, not this year,
but the next—someone who is very close to
the chief of staff told me so.

Don't you think they'll want to get
to the bottom of it right away?

I noticed, not without a slight
shock to the heart, the words
"Simonet and family" on the first
page of the arrivals list.

49

We left for dinner at Rivebelle.

Won't you be cold?
Perhaps it would be better to keep it—
it's not very warm tonight.

No, no.

For the time being, I was a new man, no longer anyone's grandson, a temporary brother of the waiters who were about to serve us, and I would not remember my grandmother again until I left.

When he finished playing, I gave the violinist two gold Louis that I had been saving up, over the course of a month, for something that had slipped my mind.

I gazed at the round tables whose innumerable groupings filled up the restaurant like so many planets, as they were depicted in the allegorical paintings of long ago.

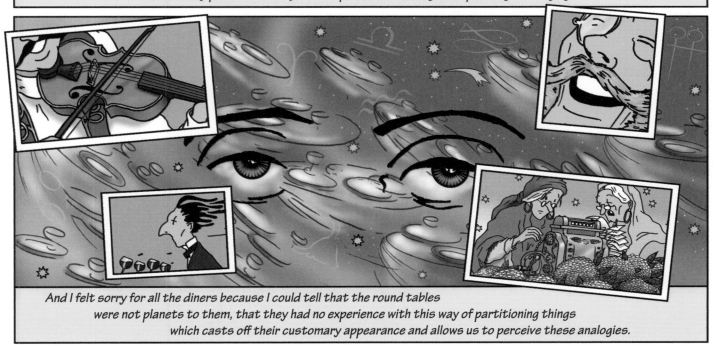

And I felt sorry for all the diners because I could tell that the round tables were not planets to them, that they had no experience with this way of partitioning things which casts off their customary appearance and allows us to perceive these analogies.

That's the young Saint-Loup. It seems he still loves his trollop. It's a real passion.

What a pretty boy!

I knew him well when I was with d'Orléans.

Oh, don't say anything, he's seen me, he's laughing, oh! He knew me all right.

I would have liked him to introduce me to these women so I could ask for a visit and have my request granted, even if I would not have been able to follow through.

If by chance to end the evening with some particular group of his friends . . .

Go on home without me, we're going to lose some Louis at the casino.

I urged the coachman to go as fast as possible.

By some contradiction that could not be concealed, it was in this moment when I experienced a singular pleasure, when I felt that my life could be happy, that I surrendered without hesitation to the chance of an accident.

I was trapped in the present, as heroes are, as drunks are;

my past was temporarily eclipsed, no longer projecting before me the shadow of itself that we call our future.

I fell into the heavy sleep that unveils before us a return to youth, the reprise of past years, the lost feelings, the disembodiment, the transmigration of souls, the summoning of the dead, the illusions of folly, the regression toward the most elemental rulings of nature.

He's had too much port.

Two o'clock!

It was a rough landing.

Messieurs Legrandin and Cambremer are brothers-in-law, aren't they?

*S*oon Saint-Loup's visit was nearing its end. I had not seen any more of those young ladies on the beach. He spent too few of his afternoons in Balbec to bother with trying, on my behalf, to make their acquaintance. In the evenings, he was more available, and he often took me with him to Rivebelle.

Who is that man dining all by himself? He always arrives when everyone else is starting to leave.

What? Don't you know Elstir, the famous painter? He once painted the cross which is at the town entrance of Rivebelle. That's it all right! You can see the four beams. Oh, it's true he takes great care!

He's a friend of Swann's and a very famous artist, a great talent.

We wrote a letter signed with both our names.

He had been one of the first to frequent this restaurant when it was still only a sort of farm, and he brought a colony of artists with him (they had all moved on as soon as the farm, where they used to eat in the open air, under a simple awning, had become an elegant meeting place. Elstir himself was only at Rivebelle that night because his wife, whom he lived with nearby, was away).

He gave me a *Sunrise over the Sea*. That must be worth a fortune, no?

Our enthusiasm for Elstir was not, as far as we could tell, from admiration,
since we had never seen anything of his. At best, it was an empty admiration.

For lack of a congenial social group, he lived in isolation, with a coarseness that
society people called a pose and bad breeding, the public authorities called an ill temper,
his neighbors madness, and his family egotism and pride.

In the few moments that Elstir came to speak with us at our table,
he never once responded to the several ways I mentioned Swann.
I started to think he didn't know him. Nevertheless, he asked me to come
see him at his Balbec studio, an invitation he didn't extend to Saint-Loup.

I promised
to visit his studio
in the next few days.

But the next day . . .

Even though, in the days before, I had mainly been thinking of the tall one, from that afternoon onward it was the girl with golf clubs, presumably Mlle Simonet herself, who preoccupied me once again.

But perhaps it was still she with the geranium complexion and green eyes whom I would have most liked to meet.

I didn't love any one of them— I loved them all.

Besides, on any given day, if the one I most wanted to glimpse wasn't there, the others would be enough to move me; my desire, though it might be directed for a moment toward this one, or that one, continued—like the first day, in my tangled vision—to bring them together; to make of them a little world apart, enlivened by a life together that of course they dared to create; and in becoming friends with one among them—like a refined pagan or a virtuous Christian among the barbarians —I would have entered into a rejuvenating society ruled by health, immorality, voluptuousness, cruelty, thoughtlessness, and joy.

It's absurd and unkind not to go see Monsieur Elstir.

But I could think of nothing but the little band.

What elegance! Every day, a new suit . . .

. . . I had even written to Paris to have new hats and ties sent.

I used every excuse to go to the beach at times I hoped I might meet them.

Stay with me a little, why don't you!

At the time, the young girls eclipsed my grandmother.

For all I knew, they were supposed to leave for America or return to Paris.
That was enough to make me start to love them. You can have a taste for someone.
But to unleash that sadness, that feeling of the irreparable,
the suffering that opens the way to love, there must be a risk of impossibility.

N the end I had to obey my grandmother, which was even more troublesome because Elstir lived rather far from the promenade, on one of the newest avenues of Balbec.

Elstir's villa was perhaps the most sumptuously ugly house I'd seen, rented in spite of that, because, of all the houses in Balbec, it was the only one which could afford him a vast studio.

Elstir's studio looked like a laboratory for a kind of new creation of the world.

Naturally, he had more than just maritime scenes from Balbec at his studio. But I could see how the charm of each painting was based on a type of metamorphosis of the things represented, similar to what, in poetry, we call metaphor.

One of his most frequent metaphors was precisely the kind that, through comparing the earth and the sea, suppressed all distinction between them.

It was, for example, through a metaphor of this type—in a painting of the harbor at Carquethuit which he had finished just a few days earlier—that Elstir prepared the mind of the viewer by using only marine terms for the little town and only urban terms for the sea.

If the whole painting gave an impression of harbors where the sea came up on land, or the land was already marine, with an amphibious population, then the force of the marine element burst out everywhere.

59

The effort Elstir made to strip himself, in the presence of reality, of all notions of his intelligence was even more admirable, for this man—who before painting, made himself ignorant, forgetting everything out of integrity (since what we know does not belong to us)—was possessed of an exceptionally cultivated intelligence.

What? The Church at Balbec?

You were disappointed in that portico?

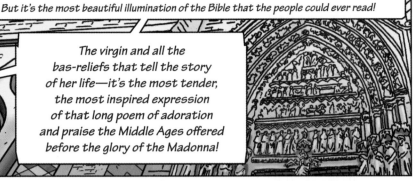

But it's the most beautiful illumination of the Bible that the people could ever read!

The virgin and all the bas-reliefs that tell the story of her life—it's the most tender, the most inspired expression of that long poem of adoration and praise the Middle Ages offered before the glory of the Madonna!

The idea of that long veil the Virgin is carried in, since she is too sacred for the angels to dare touching her directly . . .

and the one who dips his hand into Jesus' bath water, to see if it's hot enough . . .

and the one coming out of the clouds . . .

and all the ones bending down from on high . . .

. . . it's all the circles of heaven, a great theological, symbolic poem you have there. It's wild, it's divine, it's a thousand times better than anything you see in Italy . . .

. . . or other places where this pediment was copied exactly by sculptors with far less genius.

Because, you must understand, all this is a question of genius. There was never a time when everyone was a genius, that's all nonsense, that would've been quite some golden age.

This vast celestial vision, this gigantic theological poem— I understood that these had been written there, but when my eyes, full of desires, had been open before the façade— this was not what I had seen.

I thought I'd find an almost Persian monument. That's probably where I went wrong.

Not at all, there's quite a bit of truth to that.

Some parts are completely oriental.

One capital so perfectly reproduces a Persian image that the prevalence of oriental traditions isn't enough to explain it.

The sculptor must have copied some trunk brought back by explorers.

?

Do you know that young lady, Monsieur?

Elstir told me her name was Albertine Simonet, and he also gave me the names of her other friends, whom I described with enough detail that he scarcely hesitated.

Not a day goes by without one or the other of them passing by the studio to pay me a little visit.

I had miscalculated when it came to their social situation.

I had assigned a dubious class to these daughters of a very rich petit bourgeois, from the world of industry and commerce.

If I had gone to see Elstir when my grandmother told me to, I probably would have met Albertine quite a bit earlier.

I could only marvel at how much the French bourgeoisie resembled a marvelous studio full of the most generous and varied sculptures.

What unexpected types, what invention in the character of faces, what precision, what freshness, what naïveté in their features! The miserly old bourgeois who had brought forth these Dianas, these nymphs, seemed to me like the greatest of sculptors.

I thought she must have gone to join her friends on the promenade. If I could have been there with Elstir, I would have been able to meet them.

I invented a thousand pretexts for him to come take a walk by the beach with me.

I'd be glad to, but first, let me finish this bit.

And so I unearthed a watercolor which must have come from a long-ago chapter of Elstir's life.

At the bottom of the portrait, a note read: "Miss Sacripant, October 1872." I couldn't contain my admiration.

Oh! That's nothing, just a rough sketch from my youth—it was a costume for a variety show. All that was ages ago.

And what became of the model?

Quick, hand me that canvas, I hear Mme Elstir coming, and even though, I assure you, this young person in a bowler hat has played no role in my life, it would be pointless for my wife to lay eyes on that watercolor.

I only kept it as an amusing example of the theater of those years.

But really I should only keep the head—the bottom is too poorly painted and the hands are a beginner's work.

I was so sorry to see Mme Elstir arrive, since she would further delay us.

She didn't stay long.

She might have been beautiful at twenty, leading an ox through the Roman countryside.

My beautiful Gabrielle!

Later, when I became familiar with Elstir's mythological paintings, Mme Elstir also became beautiful to me.

What tricks I played to make Elstir linger in the spot where I thought those young girls might still pass by!
I thought we might have better luck catching the little band if we went down to the far end of the beach.

. . . tell me about Carquethuit.

Ah !

. . . how I'd love to go to Carquethuit . . .

. . . without realizing that the element of originality that was so powerfully apparent in Elstir's Carquethuit Harbor might have more to do with the painter's vision than with any special merits of that beach.

Evening was falling; it was time to return;

All of a sudden, like Mephistopheles rising up before Faust . . .

Feeling that the meeting between us and them was happening, and that Elstir would call me over, I turned my back like a bather about to be caught by the swell.

I hung back, peering into the window of an antiques dealer.

I studied the storefront while I waited for the moment when my name, called out by Elstir, would strike me like an expected and inoffensive shot.

Now that it was inevitable, the pleasure of meeting them felt compromised, reduced.

Elstir would surely call me over.

?!

All was lost.

I would have been so glad to meet them.

So why did you stay so far away?

I was telling you about Carquethuit. I made a little drawing where you can see the contours of the beach much more clearly.

If you'll permit me, as a souvenir of our friendship, I'll give you my sketch.

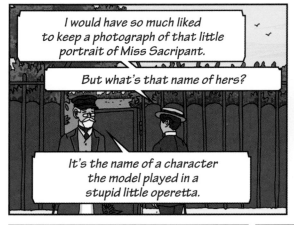

I would have so much liked to keep a photograph of that little portrait of Miss Sacripant.

But what's that name of hers?

It's the name of a character the model played in a stupid little operetta.

But you must understand, Monsieur, I didn't know her at all—

You seem to think otherwise.

But isn't that Mme Swann, before her marriage?

These brusque, fortuitous meetings with the truth, though altogether rather rare, are enough, in retrospect, to give a certain basis to the theory of premonitions.

Elstir did not answer. It was in fact a portrait of Odette de Crécy. She had not wanted to keep it.

Was it possible that this man of genius used to be the perverse and ridiculous painter the Verdurins had once adopted?

I asked him if he had known them, if by chance they had nicknamed him M. Biche.

Without embarrassment, he told me it was true, as if he was not aware of the disappointment it had awakened in me, but raising his eyes, he read it on my face.

Since you've been to this show, Monsieur Biche, I'd like you to tell me if there's really more in these late works than the virtuosity that was already so stunning . . .

. . . I went up close to see how it was done. I put my nose right up against it. And yes,

He's so funny that Biche!

. . . it was impossible to tell whether it was done with glue, red wax, soap, leaven, sunshine, or shit!

Instead of saying something which could have avenged his self-respect, he chose words that might instruct me:

There is no man, wise though he may be, who has not, at some point in his youth, spoken words or even led a life whose memory is disagreeable to him, which he wishes he could obliterate . . .

. . . there's no more chance of discovering how it was done than there is in The Night Watch . . .

. . . and the brushwork is as bold as Rembrandt's . . .

Ooooh! . . .

. . . it smells good, it makes you dizzy, it takes your breath away, you feel tingles down your spine and not the faintest clue how it's done . . .

it's witchcraft, it's cunning, it's a miracle:

it's dishonest!

. . . and yet so honest!

. . . I know there are young people whose tutors school them in nobility of spirit and moral elegance, but these are meagre characters, feeble descendants of rule-followers whose wisdom is sterile.

You cannot receive wisdom—you have to discover it for yourself.

I took my leave of Elstir.

I was disappointed not to have made the girls' acquaintance. But now there was at least a possibility that I might somehow encounter them.

The following days were occupied by preparations for Saint-Loup's departure.

By carriage or rail, it will be about the same.

So be it, I'll take the little "dawdler."

My grandmother had been wanting to tell my friend how grateful she was for the kindness he had shown us both.

These are signed letters from Proudhon.

Take them, they're for you, I had them sent here to give to you.

The next day . . .

I didn't thank your grandmother enough.

I promise to come see you several times a week.

Yes, you can come to lunch, to dinner, or even come live at Doncières.

You too, if you're ever passing by Doncières one afternoon when I have some free time, you can ask for me in the neighborhood,

but in truth, I'm almost never free.

So, when should we go?

After all his amiability, it would be rude on my part not to take him up on his invitation.

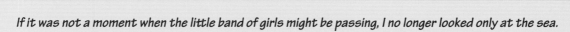
If it was not a moment when the little band of girls might be passing, I no longer looked only at the sea.

I tried to find beauty where I never imagined it to be,
in the most ordinary objects, the profound life of "nature mortes."

A FEW days after Saint-Loup's departure, when I had succeeded in convincing Elstir to host a little gathering where I might meet Albertine, I regretted that the charm and elegance I displayed as I left the hotel had not been reserved for the conquest of some other, more interesting person. My mind found this pleasure much less precious, now that it was assured.

When I arrived at Elstir's, I thought at first that Mlle Simonet was not at the studio.

There was, in fact, a young lady sitting down . . . but . . .

. . . I could not find the image I had distilled of a young cyclist riding along the sea, a cloth cap on her head.

But it was Albertine.

Even when I realized it, I paid no attention to her.

By entering any social gathering,

when you are young,

. . . you become lost to yourself, you become a different man, every parlor seems a new universe where, following the law of another moral perspective, you shine the beams of your attention as if they had to make a lasting impression upon people, dances, groups of card-players that you will have forgotten the next day.

Come, let me introduce you!

I found myself lending the same importance to these different episodes that I lent to my introduction to Mlle Simonet.

Which is not to say that the meeting which followed gave me no pleasure . . .

I did not naturally feel pleasure until a bit later, when, after returning to the hotel alone, I became myself again. There are pleasures which resemble photography. What you get in the presence of the beloved is just a snapshot negative—you must develop it later, in your own home, when you are at liberty to find the dark interior room whose entrance is forbidden in social circumstances.

The moment our names echo in the mouth of the person introducing us—especially if, like Elstir, they surround those names with elegiac embellishments—this sacramental moment,

akin to the moment in a fairy tale, when the genie orders a person to suddenly become someone else—the girl vanishes whom we once desired to approach.

As I drew toward the young girl and began to know her better, this knowledge was gotten by subtraction. Her name, her parentage—these had been the first limitations put before my imaginings. Her friendliness was another barrier. Finally, I was astonished to hear her use the adverb "perfectly" instead of "altogether"—

she's perfectly batty, but very nice all the same . . .

As unpleasant as I found this use of "perfectly," it did imply a certain degree of civilized culture . . .

he's a perfectly common, perfectly boring gentleman…

that I could not have imagined for this maenad on a bicycle, this orgiastic muse of golf.

To conclude this first evening of our acquaintance, seeking to remember the little beauty mark on her cheek beneath her eye, I was aware that, at Elstir's, after Albertine had left, I imagined that the mark must be on her chin. All told, I had noticed her beauty mark when I saw her, but my errant memory let it wander across Albertine's face, placing it sometimes here and sometimes there.

One morning, a short while later . . .

What weather! Balbec's endless summer is nothing but a joke!

Remembering how I was struck by her "cultured ways," she astonished me to the contrary with her harsh tone and her "little band" manners.

Don't you do anything here? We never see you on the golf course, or at the casino dances; and you don't go riding either. You must be bored silly!

Don't you find it stupefying dull to stay on the beach all day?

Oh! Maybe you like to bask like a lizard? You must have a lot of free time. You must not be like me— I love all sports!

Haven't you been to the races at Sogne? We went there on the tram, and I don't think you would have liked riding a clunker like that! We were on there for two hours! I could have made it there and back three times on my bike.

Though I had admired Saint-Loup when he had, with complete naturalness, called the little local train the "dawdler" because of the innumerable twists and turns it made, I was intimidated by Albertine's ease in calling the tram a "clunker."

The beauty mark—which I had remembered sometimes on the cheek, sometimes on the chin— now rested permanently above the upper lip, beneath the nose.

But won't your friends complain if you leave them . . .

Not at all, they don't need me.

Coming from the golf club, Octave?

Oh! It sickens me really, I gummed it all up.

Was Andrée there?

Yes, she scored seventy-seven.

Oh! That must be a record!

You mind?

I was struck by how far this young man had been able to develop his knowledge about all kinds of garments, how to wear them, cigars, English drinks, horses—all in isolation, devoid of the least bit of intellectual culture.

His father is a very wealthy industrialist— the president of the landowners' association in Balbec.

You could have introduced me!

But come now! I can't introduce you to a gigolo!

This place is bursting with gigolos. But they shouldn't be chatting with you. This particular one plays golf very well, full stop. I know him, he's not at all your type.

Who is that Ostrogoth over there?

Excuse me, but I just wanted to let you know that I'm going to Doncières tomorrow. It would be impolite to wait any longer, and I'm already wondering what Saint-Loup-en-Bray must think of me.

I told Bloch I could not go.

Well then, I'll go alone.

I admit that he's a rather handsome boy, but how he disgusts me!

I had never imagined that Bloch could be a handsome boy, but he was, of course.

That's my friend Bloch.

I would've bet he was a yid. It's just like them to be slimy.

We parted, Albertine and I, but agreed to go out together sometime. I had talked to her without knowing where I scattered my words.

I promised myself that the next time I saw Albertine, I would be bolder, but what I said was quite different from my plan.

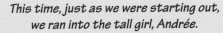
This time, just as we were starting out, we ran into the tall girl, Andrée.

Albertine was forced to introduce me.

Five gentlemen passed by whom I had come to recognize during my time in Balbec. I had often wondered who they were.

Those aren't very chic people. The little old man there, dyed hair, with the yellow gloves, he's got a way about him, you know, he's very well turned out, that's Balbec's dentist, he's a good man;

The fat one is the mayor;

Not the fat little one, he's the dancing instructor. He won't tolerate us because we make too much noise at the casino.

And M. de Saint-Croix is with them, the general councilor who joined up with the Republicans to make some money.

The thin one is the conductor of the orchestra. Have you heard the *Cavalleria Rusticana*? Oh! I thought it was marvelous! He's hosting a concert this evening,

. . . but we can't go because its taking place at the town hall. If it was at the casino, it would be something else, but at the town hall, where they've taken down the crucifix . . .

You must be thinking that my aunt's husband is in the government. But what can I do? My aunt is my aunt—I don't have to like her! She's only ever wanted one thing: to get rid of me.

Ah! Do you know the little d'Ambresac girls? They're very nice but so well brought up that they aren't allowed to go to the casino.

They're just a couple of lily-white geese.

It seems that they're pleasing enough, since one of them is already engaged to the Marquis de Saint-Loup.

Their way of lisping their words is enough to drive me mad. Besides, their outfits are ridiculous.

If you want an elegant woman, just look at Madame Elstir.

Oh really? She seemed very simply dressed to me.

She doesn't wear anything fussy, it's true, but she has a delightful style.

Albertine felt a great admiration for Elstir and knew his paintings in a way that sharply contrasted her admiration for the *Cavalleria Rusticana.*
Her taste for painting had almost surpassed her taste in clothes.

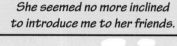

She seemed no more inclined to introduce me to her friends.

It's very good of you to bother with them. Don't pay them any mind, it's nothing at all.

At least Andrée is remarkably intelligent. She's a good little girl, if perfectly fanciful, but the others are really quite stupid.

All of a sudden, I felt very sorry that Saint-Loup had hidden his engagement from me, and that he would stoop to marrying without first breaking off from his mistress.

On one of the following mornings . . .

Hello—may I join you?

Albertine, who was perhaps irritated to see her bareheaded, responded with a glacial silence, but in spite of this, the other girl stayed, kept at a distance by Albertine who arranged to be alone with her at certain moments, and at others walked with me, so that the girl was left behind.

I was obliged to ask
Albertine for an introduction
in front of the other girl.

And I saw the glowing flash of a
friendly, affectionate smile.

She immediately blushed, and I thought
she must be shy when she liked someone

and that it was for me, out of love for me,
that she had lingered with us.

But the words promised in Gisèle's gaze could not be spoken because Albertine,
stubbornly standing between us, replied more and more curtly, before ceasing to respond at all
to what her friend was saying, and the girl was forced to take her leave.

You weren't very nice to her.

That will teach her
to be more discreet.

Why did she glom on to us like that?

Besides, I hate
the way she had her
hair—it makes
a bad impression.

I hadn't
noticed that.

Well you certainly
looked at her enough!
One would think
you wanted to
paint her portrait.

In any case, she's run out of time
to reap what she sows—
she's about to go back to Paris.

She has to cram for her exams,
the poor kid.

I went back to the hotel, ordered a coach,
and had him drive me to the train station.

Gisèle would not be too
surprised to see me there.

On the Paris train, there was a corridor between compartments where I could lead Gisèle into shadowed corners while the "Miss" slept,

and arrange to meet with her as soon as I could, when I returned to Paris.

All the same, what would she have thought if she knew that I had long hesitated between her and her friends, that I had just as much wanted to be in love with Albertine,

with the bright-eyed girl, and with Rosemonde!

I felt some remorse,

now that a requited love would unite me with Gisèle.

A few days later, despite Albertine's reluctance to introduce us, I had become acquainted with the whole "little band" from the first day, plus a few other girls they knew who had asked to meet me.

Before long, I spent every day with those girls.

Alas! In the freshest flower, one can make out the faintest points which reveal, to the trained eye, what will become the immutable and already predestined form of the seed.

One had only to see these young girls next to a mother or an aunt to measure the distances their features, swayed by some inward force that follows a frightful type, would travel in less than thirty years . . .

As on a plant whose flowers ripen at different moments, I had seen, in the old women on the Balbec beach, those hard seeds, those folded tubers, which my friends would one day become.

But what did it matter? This was the season of flowers.

We often saw Bloch's sisters.

I'm not allowed to play with "Israelites."

These young bourgeois girls from devout families had no difficulty believing that Jews sometimes slit the throats of Christian children.

Besides, your friends have dirty manners . . .

. . . like everything related to their tribe.

One of the cousins scandalized the casino by openly admiring Mlle Léa,

. . . whom the elder M. Bloch prized highly for her talent as an actress, but whose taste was not especially directed toward the gentlemen . . .

Though she had seemed chilly at first, Andrée was infinitely more delicate, more affectionate, and more refined than Albertine, to whom she displayed the soothing sweetness of a tender older sister.

Well then, Andrée what are you waiting for? You know we're going to tea at the golf club.

No, I'm staying to talk with him.

But you know Mme Durieux invited you!

Come now, sweet girl—don't be so silly.

Have it your way! But I've got to trot—I'm sure your watch is slow.

She's charming, but impossible.

If, in her taste for amusements, Albertine had something in common with Gilberte in the early days, it was due to a certain resemblance that exists, even as it evolves, between the last woman and the next we love.

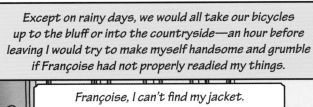

Except on rainy days, we would all take our bicycles up to the bluff or into the countryside—an hour before leaving I would try to make myself handsome and grumble if Françoise had not properly readied my things.

Françoise, I can't find my jacket.

It's because I put it on a hanger rather than just leaving it to gather dust . . .

I don't understand how anyone could leave their things like that

and just you see if anyone else could make sense of this mess. The Devil himself would be baffled.

Oh, if it were up to me, I'd take a very different vacation in Balbec!

Here are the cheese and salad sandwiches that you had prepared.

And did you buy the tarts?

Yes.

And they could very well take turns paying for them if they weren't so selfish.

We started out.

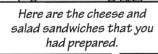

At one time, I would have wanted this ride to take place in bad weather.
I had tried to find, in Balbec, that "land of Cimmerians," and the beautiful days
were something that should not have existed there, an intrusion of bathers
and vulgar summer upon the misty veils of that ancient realm.

But now, everything that I had once disdained
and banished from my sight—not only the sun's
effects, but even the regattas, the horse races—
I passionately sought it out . . .

I only saw Elstir with the girls
when we sometimes went to visit him,

and he tended to show us
a few studies of pretty yachtswomen . . .

How things are transformed in the luminous immensity of a racetrack,
where you find so many surprising shadows and glints

only visible there!

The first meet was especially marvelous,

Or else a sketch done
at an arena near Balbec.

. . . a light like this . . . oh, how
I would have liked to capture it.

And the regattas!

He was even more
enthusiastic about yacht
races than about horses,

and I understood that, for a modern artist, regattas
and sporting events could be as interesting as the parties that
Véronèse and Carpaccio were so taken with rendering.

Your comparison is even more apt
because, in the city where they painted, those
parties had a nautical element.

But look, here's a young lady who already understands what the hat and parasol were like.

How I'd like to be rich enough for a yacht! What beautiful trips I'd take!

And an automobile.

Do you think women's fashions for automobiles are pretty?

No, but they will be. Besides, there are very few real dressmakers, one or two, Callot, Doucet, Cheruit, sometimes Paquin. The rest are atrocious.

Is there really such a difference?

It's huge, my good little man.

Oh! Sorry.

Perfectly true, without going so far as to say it's as great as the difference between a statue from the Reims Cathedral and one from the Church of Saint Augustin.

And speaking of cathedrals, the other day I described the church at Balbec to you as a great cliff, but inversely, look at these cliffs.

It's a sketch I made nearby, at Creuniers.

... Look at how the powerful, delicate carving of the rocks evokes a cathedral.

Albertine and Andrée insisted that I'd been there a hundred times. In that case, it was without my knowledge, and without knowing that one day the sight of them would awaken in me such a thirst for beauty.

THERE were days when we ate at one of the farm restaurants nearby. There were the farms called the Écorres, Marie-Thérèse, the Croix-d'Herland, the Bagatelle, the California, and the Marie-Antoinette.

The little band had adopted this last one.

But sometimes, instead of going to a farm, we climbed to the top of the bluff.

Between the close-together faces, the air that separated them traced azure pathways like the ones teased out by a gardener who wanted to let in a little daylight so that he himself could circulate among the thicket of roses.

For the most part, even the faces of these young girls were blurred by the murky blush of dawn, when the true features had not yet emerged.

It happens so fast—the moment when you have nothing left to wait for, when the body is fixed in an arrangement that has no more surprises in store.

This radiant morning is so brief, that you come to love only the youngest girls.

I delighted in listening to their chirps.

Like older people lack a gland that infants possess, whose juices help them digest milk, so too did the clucking of these young girls contain notes that were absent from the voices of women.

Once our provisions were exhausted, we played games that had once seemed boring to me.

"King of the Castle!"

No! "Who Laughs First!"

80

It wasn't just a society morning, a walk with Mme de Villeparisis, that I sacrificed to play "Ferret of the Woods" or "What Am I?" with my friends:

While spending time with Mme de Villeparisis or Saint-Loup, I would have expressed, in my speech, much more pleasure than I felt, but when I reclined among these young girls, the fullness of my feelings prevailed over the poverty, the scarcity of our speech, and brimmed over in waves of joy whose lapping ripples exhausted themselves at the feet of these young roses.

One day . . .

Does someone have a pencil?

Andrée did, and Rosemonde offered paper.

My good little women, you are forbidden to peek at what I'm writing.

Take care that no one sees.

But instead of silly scribblings,

I should show you the letter I got from Gisèle this morning.

Gisèle must have thought she should send her friend the composition she had written for her diploma.

Subject: "From the shades, Sophocles writes to Racine to console him after the failure of Athalie."

It's with Albertine that I'll have my novel.

One afternoon we were playing Ferret of the Woods . . .

I gazed with envy at the young man who was Albertine's neighbor, thinking that if I was in his place, I would have been able to touch my friend's hands during these unexpected minutes which might never transpire again.

Just the mere contact of Albertine's hands already seemed delicious to me.
The pressure of her hand had a sensual softness. This pressure seemed to let you
enter the young girl, to enter the depths of her senses, like the timbre of her laughter,
indecent as cooing or as certain cries.

On purpose, I let myself be caught with the ring, and once in the center,
I pretended not to see when it moved, following it with my eyes and waiting
for the moment when it would arrive in the hands of Albertine's neighbor.

We really are in the lovely woods . . .

"He passed this way, my lady, the ferret of the woods,

he came this way, good lady, the ferret of the bonny woods."

You have hair like Laura Dianti, or like Eléonore de Guyenne and her descendant who was much loved by Chateaubriand.

You should always let a few locks hang down.

Players of both sexes began to wonder at my ineptitude and why I did not take the ring.

All of a sudden, the ring passed to Albertine's neighbor.

Right away . . .

He had to take my place at the center of the circle, and I took his spot next to Albertine.

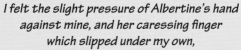

I felt the slight pressure of Albertine's hand against mine, and her caressing finger which slipped under my own,

She's using the game to show how much she likes me.

. . . and in the same moment I saw her try to wink at me without the others noticing.

Come on, take it—I've been trying to pass it to you for an hour!

The ferret noticed the ring,

And I had to go back to the middle.

We can't play when someone doesn't pay attention and tries to make other people lose.

We won't invite him anymore on days when we play, Andrée, or else I won't come at all.

Andrée tried to distract me from Albertine's rebukes.

We're just steps from those Creuniers that you wanted to see so badly.

Listen, I'll take you there on a pretty little path while these foolish girls finish acting like eight-year-olds.

Since Andrée was so very kind to me, as we walked, I told her everything about Albertine that might encourage her to love me.

She replied that she also liked her very much; but my compliments about her friend did not seem to bring her pleasure.

All of a sudden . . .

?

I stopped short, touched to the heart by a sweet memory from childhood.

I recognized a hawthorn bush, stripped of its flowers since the end of spring.

Around me floated an atmosphere of old May-times on Sunday afternoons.

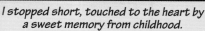
Andrée, with a charming perceptiveness, left me to commune for a moment with the leaves of the shrub.

I caught up with Andrée and began to praise Albertine once more.

It seemed impossible that she would not repeat my words to her.

And yet I never learned if Albertine heard them.

As I listened to the charming things she said about a possible affection between me and Albertine, it seemed that she should have been working hard to bring it about.

Albertine was incapable of the thousand refinements of goodness Andrée possessed, and yet I was not certain of the deep goodness of the second, the way I later became convinced of the first.

Look, there are your famous Creuniers, and how lucky you are to be seeing them in the same light as Elstir's painting.

But I was still crestfallen to have plunged, during the game of ferret, from such high hopes.

A few days after the game, we had let ourselves wander too far on a walk, and had been very happy to find a couple of little "rattletraps" with two seats...

Rosemonde can ride with me

or maybe Andrée . . .

... I led everyone to think, as if it were against my will, that I was stuck with Albertine, in whose company I feigned to be somehow resigned.

In the week that followed, I never sought out Albertine's company. I pretended to prefer Andrée.

When I spoke to Andrée about Albertine, I affected a coldness which was perhaps less convincing to Andrée than she led me to believe.

I'm well aware that you like Albertine, that you're bending over backward to get closer to her circle.

About a month after the game of ferret . . .

Albertine has to visit her aunt, Mme Bontemps, for a few days; someone told me that since she has to take an early train, she'll stay at the Grand Hotel the night before.

I don't believe it one bit.

Besides, it won't help you at all, since I'm certain that Albertine won't want to see you if she's at the hotel alone.

It wouldn't be good protocol.

But what do you think it matters to me if you see her or not?

I don't care either way.

We were joined by Octave . . .

and then by Albertine . . .

I heard that Mme de Villeparisis has been complaining to your father about diabolos on the promenade

. . . she got hit in the face with one.

Yes. It's ridiculous. There are already so few entertainments here.

I don't know why that woman made such a fuss —that old lady Mme Cambremer got hit too, and you don't hear her complaining.

He left, and then so did Andrée. I was alone with Albertine.

Don't you see, I do my hair the way you like it now, just look at my curls. No one has guessed who I've been doing it for. My aunt will tease me like everyone else, but I won't tell her either.

I asked her if the plans I had heard about were true:

Yes, I'll be spending that night at your hotel, and what's more, I'll go to bed before dinner, since I have a bit of a cold. You can sit by my bed while I have dinner, and then afterward we can play whatever you like.

Come early,

that way we'll have a few good hours together.

I went to dinner with my grandmother. I could feel a secret inside me that she did not know.

What was about to happen was still a mystery to me.

87

In any case, the Grand Hotel, the evening, no longer seemed empty—it contained all my happiness.

Those few steps from the landing to Albertine's room, those steps that no one could now prevent, I undertook them with delight, and with care.

Then, all of a sudden, it occurred to me that I was wrong to have doubts, that she had told me to come to her when she would be in bed.

Her cheek was spanned top to bottom by one of those long, black tresses, a curl that she had left entirely undone to please me.

I was about to know the smell, the taste of that pink, unknown fruit.

Seeing that I was leaning down to kiss her . . .

STOP OR I'LL RING !

But I told myself that it wasn't for nothing that a young girl would invite a young man to her lair . . .

Briiing!

Briiing! Briiing! Briiing! Briiing!

Albertine had rung with all her might.

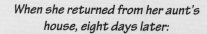

When she returned from her aunt's house, eight days later:

I forgive you, I even regret having caused you pain, but don't ever do that again.

My dreams, which I had thought were independent, abandoned her just as soon as they ceased to be nourished by the hope of possession. From then on, they found themselves free, once again, to settle on this or that friend of Albertine's.

She was certainly sorry to have been unable to please me and gave me a little gold pencil.

You bring me great pleasure, however less it may be than the pleasure I might have known if you had allowed me to kiss you.

. . . that would have made me so happy, and what harm would it have done you? I'm shocked that you refused me.

If my conduct surprised you, I wonder what sort of young girls you must have known.

To me, these kinds of things have no importance . . .

. . . to allow oneself to be kissed, and what's more, by a friend, since you say I am your friend . . .

You are, but I've had others before you.

And well, not one of them would have dared to do something like that.

They know I'd have slapped them silly.

But I'm sure that you don't care about me. Admit it— Andrée is the one you like.

When it comes down to it, you're right—she's much nicer than I am, and why, she's gorgeous!

Ah! Men!

During the long hours I spent chatting, taking tea, and playing with these young girls, I had even forgotten

that they were the same pitiless and sensual virgins that I had seen parading before the sea, like in a fresco.

And in the end, this is a way, like any other, of resolving the problem of existence—to get close enough to the things and the people which have seemed mysterious and beautiful to us from afar, to understand that they are without mystery and without beauty;

this is one regimen among many, a regimen that is perhaps a bit discouraged, but it does give us a certain calm in which to spend our lives, and to resign ourselves to our deaths.

Albertine left first, abruptly.

She didn't give any rhyme or reason, and now she's gone.

My friends left Balbec, not all together, but in the same week.

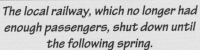

The local railway, which no longer had enough passengers, shut down until the following spring.

There aren't enough means of commotion here.

I didn't have sufficient support.

You'll see next year what a phalanx I'll be able to roust.

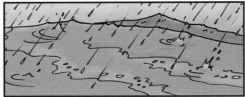

Since the casino had closed, the driving rain sometimes kept my grandmother and me shut up in rooms that were nearly empty, as in the depths of a ship's hold, when the wind is blowing.

The presiding judge from Rennes, a head of bar from Caen, an American woman and her daughters, came to us, starting a conversation, inventing ways to make the hours pass more quickly, revealing a talent . . .

In short, I had scarcely benefited from my time in Balbec, which only strengthened my desire to return.

Next year, I'll save you the best rooms.

But I was attached to my own, which I now entered without noticing the whiff of vetiver.

We should have left Balbec—the cold and the damp had become too overpowering.
Besides, I immediately forgot those last few weeks.

WHAT I would invariably picture when I thought of Balbec were the moments when, each morning during the high season, before my excursions with Albertine and her friends in the afternoons, my grandmother would force me, on doctor's orders, to stretch out in darkness.

I knew my friends were on the promenade, but I could not see them. I divined their presence, I heard their enveloping laughter like the laughter of Nereids in the gentle swell which climbed to reach my ears.

I kept the tall purple curtains closed, but despite the pins Françoise used to bind them, despite the fabric added here and there to adjust them, the darkness was not total.

Noon would come, Françoise would arrive at last.

We looked to see if you would come down. But your shutters were closed, even when the concert began.

The summer day she uncovered seemed just as dead, just as timeless as a sumptuous, thousand-year-old mummy that our old servant had merely unswaddled from all its linens before revealing it, embalmed in its golden robe.

GLOSSARY

p. 28

Saumur: the location of the French cavalry school for which Saint-Loup is preparing.

p. 28

Doncières: a fictional town with a training garrison.

p. 29

*Proudhon: Pierre-Joseph Proudhon (1809–1865) was a provocative writer
and journalist with far-left views, including variations on anarchism.*

p. 32

*Amphitrite: in Greek mythology, she is the sea god Poseidon's consort and queen.
Her name also serves as an evocation of the sea itself.*

p. 38

*Andromaque and Phèdre: these are both tragic plays by Racine and important parts of the French canon.
Each play borrows characters from Greek mythology who were also brought to life in the plays of Euripides.*

p. 39

*Le Nôtre: André Le Nôtre (1613–1700) was a landscape architect and the principal gardener for King Louis XIV at Versailles.
His work is a prime example of aristocratic gardens. Like Nicolas Poussin's paintings, Le Nôtre's gardens relied on order and line to
give a formal, cultivated impression.*

p. 40

*Bergotte: a fictional author who appears in several volumes of In Search of Lost Time. The narrator admires his novels
and uses this character as a foil, or a window, into his own writing practice.*

PART TWO
p. 64

*Mme Swann, Odette de Crécy: the wife of Charles Swann, mother of Gilberte, and formerly a demimondaine and mistress
to several aristocratic men. She is the subject of Swann's obsession and jealousy in Swann's Way, and his marriage to her is
considered vulgar by other members of high society. It is implied that Elstir was perhaps also enamored of her, but perhaps
his feelings were not returned, since she did not keep the portrait he painted of her.*

p. 64

The Night Watch: a painting by Rembrandt.

p. 65

"Nature mortes": the French term for a "still life"—an arrangement of nonliving objects used by artists to create a composition.

p. 71

*Cavalleria Rusticana: a popular one-act opera by Pietro Mascagni, which the narrator views as crass and unsophisticated. The title
means "rustic chivalry," and the opera takes as its subject a love triangle between a returning soldier and two women in his village.*

p. 75

*"openly admiring Mlle Léa": Like the Baron de Charlus, Mlle Léa is another one of Proust's characters who is rumored to be
homosexual. When Bloch's sisters admire her, it puts them even more at odds with the aristocratic traditions of the setting.*

Véronèse and Carpaccio: Paolo Véronèse (1528–1588) and Vittore Carpaccio (1465–1520) were two Italian Renaissance painters who depicted the gorgeous textiles of high Venetian style.

Athalie: the last tragedy written by Racine, which is now regarded as a masterpiece, though its initial public reception was quite negative.

Laura Dianti and Eléonore de Guyenne: both women were prominent medieval beauties. The lover of the Duke of Ferrara, Laura Dianti was immortalized by her portrait painted by Titian. Eléonore de Guyenne, better known as Eleanor of Aquitaine, was a famous queen of both England and France in the twelfth century and a creator of the "court of love" in Poitiers.

Hawthorn bush and May-times: May has traditionally been the "month of Mary" in the Catholic church, with many devotions to Mary taking place on Mother's Day and throughout the month. One particular ritual is the "May Crowning," when statues of the Virgin are adorned with flowers or other decorations. The hawthorn plant, which was often called "May" because of the moment when it flowers, has been associated with Christ, and there is a legend that his crown of thorns was made from hawthorn. However, the plant also has earlier pagan associations with the Green Man, the deity of spring's return and the cycle of seasonal death and rebirth. Because it traditionally blooms in May, the hawthorn is a symbol of the courtship rituals surrounding that time of year.

Nereids: in Greek mythology, the Nereids are sea nymphs who accompany Poseidon and carry his trident. They represent the beautiful qualities of the sea.

THE NARRATOR'S FAMILY TREE

AUNT FLORA

AUNT CÉLINE

GRANDMOTHER (BATHILDE)

GRANDFATHER (AMÉDÉE)

UNCLE ADOLPHE

GREAT-AUNT

FATHER

MOTHER

AUNT LÉONIE OR "MADAME OCTAVE" (OCTAVE'S WIDOW)

THE NARRATOR

FRANÇOISE

CHARLES SWANN

MME SWANN (ODETTE DE CRÉCY)

GILBERTE SWANN, DAUGHTER OF SWANN AND ODETTE

MARQUISE DE VILLEPARISIS

THE MARQUIS DE SAINT-LOUP-EN-BRAY

ALBERTINE SIMONET

ANDRÉE

ALBERT BLOCH

PALAMÈDE DE GUEREMANTES, BARON DE CHARLUS (KNOWN AS "MÉMÉ")

ELSTIR (KNOWN AS THE PAINTER "M. BICHE")

MANAGER OF THE
GRAND HOTEL

MLLE STERMARIA

M. STERMARIA

LEGRANDIN

OWNER OF THE GRAND HOTEL

MARQUIS DE
CAMBREMER

MARQUISE DE
CAMBREMER

PRINCESS DE
LUXEMBOURG

AIMÉ

MAÎTRE D' AT THE
RIVEBELLE RESTAURANT

GISÈLE

ROSEMONDE

OTHER MEMBERS OF THE "LITTLE BAND"

SIDONIE
VERDURIN

GUSTAVE (OR
AUGUSTE) VERDURIN

THE WRITER
BERGOTTE

OCTAVE

THE D'AMBRESAC
GIRLS

HOTEL
CONCIERGE

THE BELLHOP

BLOCH'S
SISTERS

Marcel Proust was born on July 10, 1871, at 96, Rue La Fontaine in the 16th Arrondissement of Paris (Auteuil district) and died at the age of 51 on November 18, 1922, at 44, Rue Hamelin, Paris XVI.

His family belonged to the wealthy upper middle class. His father, Adrien Proust, was a respected physician and professor of medicine and inspector general of international health. Marcel began frequenting aristocratic salons at a young age and led the life of a society dilettante, in the course of which he met numerous artists and writers.

He wrote articles, poems, and short stories (collected as *Les Plaisirs et les Jours*), as well as pastiches and essays (collected as *Pastiches et Mélanges*) and translated John Ruskin's *Bible of Amiens*. In 1895 he began a first novel, *Jean Santeuil*, which he abandoned and which was not published until 1952. Then, in 1907, he began writing *In Search of Lost Time*, of which seven volumes appeared between 1913 and 1927.

The first of these volumes, *Swann's Way*, is composed of three parts: "Combray," "Swann in Love," and "Place Names: The Name."

The second volume, *In the Shadow of Young Girls in Flower*, won the Prix Goncourt in 1919, and the final three volumes were published posthumously.

All of the *Search* is told in the first person, except for "Swann in Love," which takes place in the Paris of the 1880s, before the narrator is born.

Of fragile health, Proust suffered all his life from severe asthma. In October 1922, on his way to visit Comte Etienne de Beaumont, he became chilled and died of a poorly treated bronchitis on November 18. He is buried in the Père-Lachaise Cemetery in Paris (Division 85).

The "Proust questionnaire"

Like "Proust's madeleine" in "Combray" and "faire catleya" (in "Swann in Love"), the "Proust questionnaire" has become part of the French vocabulary. Proust was not the author, however. The questionnaire comes from an English game called "Confessions," in which Proust took part at least twice: at age thirteen in the album of Antoinette Faure and again at age twenty. The questions (and answers) were similar both times but not identical. Both versions can be consulted online through the Kolb Proust archives at the University of Illinois at Urbana-Champaign.

Proust's Family Tree

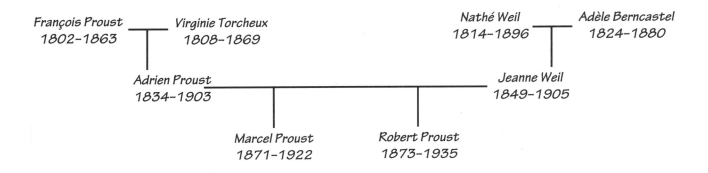

François Proust
1802–1863

Virginie Torcheux
1808–1869

Nathé Weil
1814–1896

Adèle Berncastel
1824–1880

Adrien Proust
1834–1903

Jeanne Weil
1849–1905

Marcel Proust
1871–1922

Robert Proust
1873–1935

Marcel's father was originally from Illiers in Eure-et-Loir, where "little Marcel" spent vacations with his aunt Élisabeth Amiot. She became Aunt Léonie in the *Search*, and Illiers inspired the fictive Combray.

In 1971, the centenary of the writer's birth, Illiers paid homage by changing its name to Iliers-Combray. It is the only village in France to have taken its name from a work of literature.

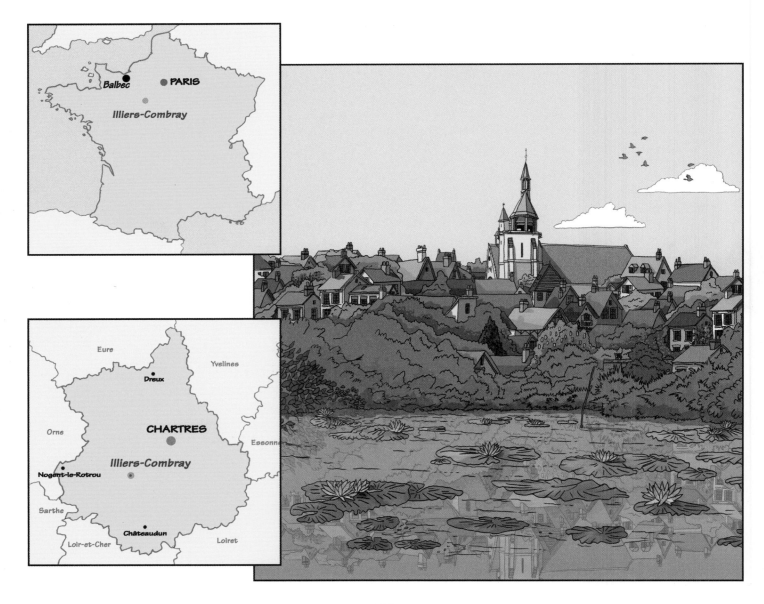